Understanding Consent and Boundaries

Dating and Relationships in the #MeToo Era

Naomi Rockler

San Diego, CA

© 2024 ReferencePoint Press, Inc.
Printed in the United States

For more information, contact:
ReferencePoint Press, Inc.
PO Box 27779
San Diego, CA 92198
www.ReferencePointPress.com

ALL RIGHTS RESERVED.
No part of this work covered by the copyright hereon may be reproduced or used in any form or by any means—graphic, electronic, or mechanical, including photocopying, recording, taping, web distribution, or information storage retrieval systems—without the written permission of the publisher.

LIBRARY OF CONGRESS CATALOGING-IN-PUBLICATION DATA

Names: Rockler, Naomi, author.
Title: Understanding consent and boundaries : dating and relationships in the #MeToo era / by Naomi Rockler.
Description: San Diego, CA : ReferencePoint Press, [2023] | Includes bibliographical references and index.
Identifiers: LCCN 2022061368 (print) | LCCN 2022061369 (ebook) | ISBN 9781678205966 (library binding) | ISBN 9781678205973 (ebook)
Subjects: LCSH: Dating (Social customs)--Juvenile literature. | Teenage girls--Attitudes--Juvenile literature. | Interpersonal relations in adolescence--Juvenile literature. | MeToo movement--Juvenile literature.
Classification: LCC HQ801 .R6245 2023 (print) | LCC HQ801 (ebook) | DDC 306.73--dc23/eng/20230110
LC record available at https://lccn.loc.gov/2022061368
LC ebook record available at https://lccn.loc.gov/2022061369

CONTENTS

Introduction   4
#MeToo and You

Chapter One   8
A Brief History of the #MeToo Movement

Chapter Two   20
Boundaries in the #MeToo Era

Chapter Three   31
Consent in the #MeToo Era

Chapter Four   42
Boundaries and Consent: How to Support Others

Source Notes	53
Ways for Supporters to Take Action	56
Organizations and Websites	58
For Further Research	59
Index	60
Picture Credits	63
About the Author	64

INTRODUCTION

#MeToo and You

When is it okay to say no? Is it okay to say no to a relative who wants a hug? Is it okay to say no to a date who wants a good night kiss?

In years past, young people—especially girls—were often taught that being polite was more important than standing up for what they wanted. These attitudes have not entirely disappeared, especially when it comes to dating and relationships. "The first time I had sex, the implication was that I would say yes," explained a college student named Courtney. "Not because I was under some form of coercion, but simply because it was the polite, lady-like thing to do."[1]

However, attitudes are changing. More than ever before, young people are speaking up unapologetically about what is acceptable and not acceptable in dating and relationships. It is *always* okay to say no. Saying no is not always easy, but learning how to stand up for oneself can feel very empowering.

In relationships, standing up for oneself involves two important concepts: boundaries and consent. Boundaries are invisible barriers that people build and tell others not to cross. Boundaries are how people communicate what behavior is acceptable and what is not acceptable. For example, someone might agree to kiss a date goodnight but say no to going further sexually.

Consent is the act of saying yes freely and willingly, without being manipulated or coerced. If a boy asks a girl for a kiss and she says yes, she has given consent. If she says no and he kisses her anyway, he has violated her consent. If she says no and he threatens to break up with her or pressures her in some other way, that is also a violation of her consent. No means no.

#MeToo, Sexual Harassment, and Sexual Assault

Today young people are talking openly about boundaries and consent in ways that were not common in previous generations. One of the reasons for this change is a cultural phenomenon called the #MeToo movement, which raised awareness of the importance of respecting boundaries and practicing consent.

The #MeToo movement started in 2017, when millions of people worldwide (mostly women, but others as well) wrote on social media about times their boundaries and consent were violated. The two topics they wrote about most, sexual harassment and sexual assault, are issues that are directly relevant to young people.

In 2017, a cultural phenomenon known as the #MeToo movement raised awareness of the importance of respecting boundaries and practicing consent.

According to the Rape, Abuse & Incest National Network (RAINN), *sexual harassment* refers to "unwelcome sexual advances, requests for sexual favors, and other verbal or physical harassment of a sexual nature in the workplace or learning environment."[2] In the workplace this includes unwanted sexual advances, unwanted conversations or jokes about sexual topics, and inappropriate touching. Sexual harassment can also happen in public places—on the street, on public transportation, or just about anywhere, including online. Public harassment like this is sometimes called street harassment.

For teenagers, sexual harassment can mean catcalling, groping in the hallways, or spreading sexual rumors about other students. It might also mean sending someone an unwanted sexually explicit message or photo or sharing someone else's explicit photo without his or her consent. According to a 2018 report by the National Sexual Violence Resource Center, approximately 56 percent of middle and high school girls reported they had been sexually harassed, and about 36 percent of girls said they had been harassed online. "It's just something high school girls know they have to deal with," says Maddy Eichenberg, a high school senior in Massachusetts. "A lot of female friend groups have a list of—or know about—high school boys who they know have been treating women in a gross way, and make sure their friends stay away from them."[3]

> "A lot of female friend groups have a list of—or know about—high school boys who they know have been treating women in a gross way, and make sure their friends stay away from them."[3]
>
> —Maddy Eichenberg, high school senior in Massachusetts

In addition to sexual harassment, a second topic many #MeToo posters wrote about was sexual assault. Sexual assault is any sexual contact that happens without the victim's consent, including kissing or touching. According to the Centers for Disease Control and Prevention, over half of women in the United States and almost a third of men have been victims of sexual assault. The term *rape* usually refers to sexual assault that includes forced penetration. In the United States about one out every four women have experienced either rape or attempted rape, and so have one out of every twenty-six men.

According to the National Sexual Violence Resource Center, almost 12 percent of US high school juniors have been raped. These numbers increase for women in their late teens and early twenties. In college, about one in four women are sexually assaulted.

Dating and Relationships in the #MeToo Era

In the #MeToo era the norms about dating and relationships are changing to reflect the importance of boundaries and consent. In healthy relationships, it is always okay to say no—and always important to accept no for an answer. Being polite is never more important than maintaining healthy boundaries and practicing mutual consent.

Healthy, consensual relationships are defined by mutual respect for each other's boundaries when it comes to sexual behavior, and other issues as well. Healthy relationships foster an environment of enthusiastic consent, where decisions about sexual activity are made without coercion or manipulation of any kind.

CHAPTER ONE

A Brief History of the #MeToo Movement

In previous generations, girls were taught to put up with a certain amount of harassment and unwanted touching from boys. Girls were told that it was okay for boys to tease them, because that means the boys like them. They were told to ignore catcalls from boys—or take them as a compliment. On dates, some boys were taught that no does not always mean no, and they were encouraged to pressure girls into being more physical than the girls wanted. If a girl was raped and she was wearing a short skirt, many people said that she was asking for it.

Unfortunately, even though these attitudes have slowly been changing, they have not gone away. "My daughter is experiencing her first bout with sexual harassment," a mother wrote on Twitter in 2017. "A boy in class told her he would rape her on the bus home from school on Thursday. She's 10."[4]

This tweet was one of many that appeared on Twitter in late 2017. It was part of the #MeToo movement, which has had a powerful impact on how people talk about boundaries and consent. This movement became popular in the late 2010s, but it actually originated two decades earlier.

The Origin of Me Too

In 1996 a young girl named Heaven found the courage to tell a camp counselor about a terrifying experience. Heaven had been sexually assaulted by her mother's boyfriend. The counselor, Tarana Burke, could see that Heaven felt ashamed. She sent the girl to a social worker. Years later, in her memoir, Burke wrote that she regretted not telling Heaven that she, too, was a sexual abuse survivor. Perhaps if Heaven had known this, she would have understood that she was not alone—and that the abuse was not her fault.

Inspired by this incident, Burke started leading programs at schools and churches in the Black community to raise awareness about sexual assault. She talked about the power of women sharing their experiences with each other. Burke explained, "I thought about how powerful it feels to not be alone. How empowering it is to know you don't have to walk a journey by yourself, to know that you're not the only one. And how inherently powerful it is to do things collectively. And that was the building block for Me Too."[5]

> "I thought about how powerful it feels to not be alone. How empowering it is to know you don't have to walk a journey by yourself, to know that you're not the only one."[5]
>
> —Tarana Burke, activist credited with first use of MeToo

This was the beginning of the use of the phrase "Me Too" to signify shared experiences with sexual assault and harassment. The use of this phrase would become common later, in 2017, after a series of events that outraged many women and emboldened them to speak out against sexual harassment and assault.

The Brock Turner Case

One event that caused outrage was the Brock Turner rape case in 2015. According to a Stanford University Department of Public Safety incident report, a student named Brock Turner sexually assaulted an unconscious woman behind a dumpster. Two graduate students caught him in the act. In 2016 a California jury found Turner guilty of three counts of sexual assault. At the sentencing hearing the victim released a long statement to the court, graphically describing the brutal attack and its devastating emotional impact.

Despite this, the judge seemed to have more sympathy for Turner than for the victim. During the trial, Turner's father argued that his son should not receive a long sentence because that would destroy his promising future as an athlete. Although prosecutors asked that Turner be sentenced to six years in prison, the judge sentenced him to six months. The victim later wrote, "The judge had given Brock something that would never be extended to me: empathy. My pain was never more valuable than his potential."[6]

The case got a great deal of publicity. Many people were infuriated by Turner's lenient sentence. As a result, California voters recalled the judge from his position.

Tarana Burke is credited as the founder of the #MeToo movement. As a sexual abuse survivor herself, she believes in the power of women sharing their troubling experiences.

Donald Trump's Presidential Campaign

Not long after the Turner case, celebrity businessperson Donald Trump ran for president against Hillary Clinton. As the *New York Times* reported months before the 2016 election, Trump had a longtime reputation for inappropriate behavior toward women and girls. Among many other things, he was accused of harassing teenage contestants when he owned the Miss Teen USA pageant.

Then, a month before the election, a 2005 video of Trump speaking to an *Access Hollywood* reporter was leaked to the media. Unaware that he was being recorded, Trump bragged that because he was a celebrity, he could kiss and touch women without their consent. "I'm automatically attracted to beautiful," said Trump. "I just start kissing them. It's like a magnet. Just kiss. I don't even wait. And when you're a star, they let you do it. You can do anything." He added, "Grab 'em by the pussy. You can do anything."[7]

Many Americans were shocked by these comments. Some believed Trump's chances for winning the election were over. Things seemed even worse for Trump two weeks later, when the Daily Beast published a report that included twenty-four sexual misconduct accusations against Trump, including an accusation by a reporter who said that Trump had raped her in a dressing room in the mid-1990s. Trump has categorically denied all of these charges.

Despite this, Trump won the presidential election on November 8, 2016. Many people felt as horrified as they had after Brock Turner's lenient sentence. To these people, it seemed that allegations of sexual harassment and assault were not being treated as serious crimes.

The Women's March

In response to Trump's election, one ordinary woman's initiative led to the largest protest to date in US history. Teresa Shook, a retired lawyer from Hawaii, thought that someone should organize a women's march to protest Trump's election. Shook started an organizing page on Facebook, and within a day, ten thousand people had joined. This page quickly became the organizing hub for the 2017 Women's March on Washington. The organizers wrote, "The Women's March on Washington will send a bold message to our new administration on their first day in office, and to the world, that women's rights are human rights. We stand together, recognizing that defending the most marginalized among us is defending all of us."[8]

Trump was inaugurated on January 20, 2017. The next day, about five hundred thousand women and their allies participated in the Women's March on Washington. At the same time, local women's marches took place in all fifty states and on every continent—even Antarctica, where scientists gathered to protest. The *Washington Post* estimated that over 4 million people participated worldwide. Many women wore hand-knitted pink caps that they called "pussy hats," as a commentary on Trump's infamously lewd statement.

Prominent politicians and celebrities gave powerful speeches at the marches that summed up the outrage of many. At the Washington, DC, march, pop legend Madonna said, "Let's march

#MeToo Around the World

The #MeToo movement has gone global. The hashtag #MeToo has been used in eighty-five different countries, with heaviest use in the United Kingdom, Canada, Australia, and India. Variations of the #MeToo hashtag have emerged in other languages, including Spanish (#YoTambién), Hebrew (#GamAni), French (#BalanceTonPorc, or "out your pig"), and Italian (#QuellaVoltaChe, or "that time when"). At a 2018 protest in South Korea, 193 women spoke about their personal experiences with sexual harassment, one after another, for 2,018 minutes.

Although the #MeToo movement has been dismissed in many countries, it has led to concrete changes in others. In 2019 catcalling (or sexually harassing women on the street) became a criminal offense in France. In 2022 the Spanish parliament passed the "only yes means yes" law, in response to several cases in which rapists were acquitted because their victims were silent and did not directly say no. Under the new Spanish law, all sex without a clear yes was redefined as rape.

together through this darkness and, with each step, know that we are not afraid, that we are not alone, that we will not back down, that there is power in our unity, and that no opposing force stands a chance in the face of true solidarity."[9]

The Harvey Weinstein Case

The final event that led up to the #MeToo movement was the Harvey Weinstein case. Weinstein was one of Hollywood's most famous and powerful film producers. For years there were rumors that he had sexually harassed and assaulted actresses. None of the women were willing to come forward for fear that Weinstein would destroy their careers.

Then in October 2017 the *New York Times* and *New Yorker* magazine both published shocking reports about Weinstein's behavior. Dozens of women, including superstars like Gwyneth Paltrow and Angelina Jolie, spoke out. Many women said the same thing: Weinstein lured women to hotel rooms by promising to discuss their careers. When the doors were closed, he aggressively demanded sexual favors from them, and in some cases he physically overpowered and raped them. To ensure their silence, Weinstein threatened retaliation if they spoke out. He pressured women into signing nondisclosure agreements, a type of legal document that prevented these women from discussing the incidents publicly.

Once again, people were furious. Here was another case of a powerful man getting away with sexual misconduct.

Alyssa Milano's Tweet

One woman who was angry was Alyssa Milano, an actress known for her roles in TV series like *Who's the Boss* and *Charmed*. In response to the scandal, Milano posted on her Twitter account, "If you've been sexually harassed or assaulted, write 'me too' as a response to this tweet." In her tweet she included an image that said, "Suggested by a friend: If all the women who have ever been

In 2017, actress Alyssa Milano (pictured) asked followers on her Twitter account to reply "me too" if they had ever been a victim of sexual abuse. Within days, the hashtag #MeToo had been used 12 million times on Facebook.

sexually harassed or assaulted wrote 'Me too' as a status, then we give people a sense of the magnitude of the problem."[10]

At the time, Milano did not know that Tarana Burke had also used the phrase "me too." However, like Burke, Milano hoped that by using these words, she would raise awareness about sexual assault and harassment.

When Milano woke up the next morning, she was flabbergasted; in response to her tweet, thousands of women had replied with the words "me too"—and more. Using the hashtag #MeToo, many women (and some men) posted firsthand accounts of their experiences with sexual harassment and assault. Within four days, the hashtag #MeToo had been used 1.4 million times on Twitter, and 12 million times on Facebook. Within a year the hashtag had been used 19 million times on Twitter, by people in eighty-five different countries.

Some of the tweets were from famous women, including Lady Gaga and Evan Rachel Wood, but most of the tweets were from everyday people. Many of the #MeToo tweeters wrote in explicit detail about their experiences with sexual assault and harassment. Some wrote that this was the first time they had shared these experiences with anyone—in some cases years after they happened. Others wrote that they had shared their experiences before but that others had not believed them or had blamed them for doing something to cause these experiences. Other tweeters emphasized how common sexual harassment and assault are. One wrote, "Don't think I know a single woman who hasn't been sexually harassed at work, school, or on the street."[11]

#MeToo, Teenagers, and Children

One of the most stunning things about the #MeToo tweets was the number of tweets written by teenagers and by adults writing about disturbing experiences they had had as teenagers. Perhaps even more stunning was the number of tweets about experiences people had had as preteens and small children. There were many tweets about sexual molestation by family members and others.

Many #MeToo tweets were about attacks that took place in public places. One woman wrote, "As a sixth grader, a group of boys held me against a wall as they pulled up my shirt to see if I stuffed my bra with Charmin or Bounty."[12] Another shared, "Crowded tram at Disney, sat a row behind my family. Man kept his hand on my thigh the whole ride, stroking the fine hair there. His friend looked on. Think I was 11 but scared to confirm dates of that trip with my mom, because I never told anyone."[13]

Other #MeToo tweets were about experiences that happened in schools. Many tweets were about girls being groped, forcibly kissed, or raped in school—in some cases by teachers. Many girls wrote about dealing with constant comments about their bodies, especially their

> "As a sixth grader, a group of boys held me against a wall as they pulled up my shirt to see if I stuffed my bra with Charmin or Bounty."[12]
>
> —A Twitter user

breasts. Other comments focused on feeling unsafe at school. "When I was in high school it was not safe for me to walk to class by myself," one student wrote. "My counselors and doctors recommended I find someone to escort me to class. Why? Because my high school let a perpetrator run around the hallways attacking me as he pleased."[14]

Parents and teachers also contributed tweets about the experiences of teenagers. One teacher wrote, "I'm a teacher in an urban high school and sexual harassment in our hallways [is] a real problem. Few girls see it as an issue, most have accepted it as a norm. Need advice on how to battle, prevent, and end this ingrained behavior."[15]

What Came Out of #MeToo?

After the storm of #MeToo posts, many victims reported their attackers to bosses, law enforcement, or the media. Many prominent men lost their jobs or had their reputations severely damaged. Among them were politicians (Michigan representative John Conyers, Minnesota senator Al Franken), journalists (*New York Times* writer Glenn Thrush), actors (Kevin Spacey, Jeffrey Tambor), and other entertainers (*Prairie Home Companion*'s Garrison Keillor). In 2020 Harvey Weinstein was sentenced to twenty-three years in prison.

After the #MeToo tweets, sexual harassment in the workplace began to be taken more seriously. In 2022 a Pew Research Center study reported that most Americans believe that sexual harassers are facing consequences more often than before #MeToo. In addition, after #MeToo, activists formed organizations like Time's Up to help victims fight back against sexual harassment. Media mogul Oprah Winfrey promoted Time's Up in a powerful speech at the Golden Globe Awards in 2018. "For too long, women have

> "For too long, women have not been heard or believed if they dare speak the truth to the power of those men. But their time is up. Their time is up."[16]
>
> —Oprah Winfrey, media mogul

As a result of the #MeToo movement, many prominent men lost their jobs or had their reputations severely damaged, and some even went to jail. Harvey Weinstein (pictured) was sentenced to twenty-three years in prison.

not been heard or believed if they dare speak the truth to the power of those men," said Winfrey. "But their time is up. Their time is up."[16]

For young people, the #MeToo movement has led to greater awareness of sexual harassment and assault in schools. An organization called Stop Assault in Public Schools started the #MeTooK12 Campaign to promote awareness of the issue and work with schools to find solutions. While many colleges and universities have had policies to prevent sexual harassment and assault for several decades, these programs are now becoming more common in middle schools and high schools. In addition, many middle schools and high schools have expanded sex education programs to include information about consent, boundaries, and sexual harassment and assault.

Perhaps most importantly, attitudes about sexual assault and harassment are changing. People are more aware that these issues are widespread—for adults and also for young people. Survivors are more likely to understand that they are not alone. People who have not been sexually harassed or assaulted have a better understanding of the impact of these issues on others in their lives.

For teenagers, dating and relationships have always been complicated—and #MeToo hasn't changed that. However, thanks to #MeToo, young people are talking about boundaries and consent in ways that previous generations have not. Young people are learning that they don't have to stand for others' behavior toward them if it makes them uncomfortable. They can

The #MeTooK12 Campaign

In response to the #MeToo movement, the organization Stop Sexual Assault in Schools began the #MeTooK12 Campaign, a program designed to raise awareness about the scope of this problem in elementary, middle, and high schools. The organization created a detailed tool kit for schools with information about the scope of the problem, ways to help victims, and strategies for making schools a safer place. As the executive director of the organization explained:

> Few people of influence understand how sexual harassment and assault devastate the lives of K–12 students, their families, and friends—beginning in elementary school; and the younger the victim, the more devastating the impact and greater vulnerability to repeated assault. Not only do the survivors' emotional and psychological scars endure long after the incidents, their social lives, education, and career dreams can be shattered.

Esther Warkov, "#MeTooK12 – Combating Rampant Sexual Harassment and Assault," Stop Sexual Assault in Schools, 2022. www.stopsexualassaultinschools.com.

set clear expectations for what's okay and not okay in relationships and can walk away from partners who do not respect their boundaries.

The many individuals who shared their #MeToo experiences have brought awareness that rape, sexual assault, and sexual harassment are common experiences and that these experiences are traumatizing and never okay. Young people are learning that if they have had these experiences, they are not alone—and that's a powerful feeling. As activist Najwa Zebian wrote in a #MeToo tweet, "When you say #metoo, you're no longer alone in the struggle to be heard. You're now part of #metoo. And we can change the world together."[17]

Chapter Two

Boundaries in the #MeToo Era

Julia Smith, a high school sophomore, was excited when her friend Peter asked her to be his girlfriend. Unfortunately, Peter did not respect Julia's boundaries. "He would often take pictures of me, even though I told him I would rather he didn't," says Julia. "One day, he asked me if I was OK with him recording a video of me saying 'I love you.' I hesitantly obliged, even though I was uncomfortable."[18] Peter also challenged the boundaries she set on her time and pressured her to spend time with him when she wanted to see her other friends.

Setting boundaries is a way for people to let others know the parts of themselves they are willing to share and the parts that are out-of-bounds. In all relationships, boundaries are important because they help keep people comfortable and feeling safe. This is especially important in dating relationships, which come with emotional risks like heartbreak and physical risks like sexual assault. Bullying prevention advocate Sherri Gordon explains, "Although boundaries are different for everyone, when done correctly, they help teens set limits with others in order to protect themselves. Setting boundaries allows teens to communicate with other people about what is OK and what is not OK with them and is essential for teen friendships and dating relationships."[19]

While boundaries are important for everyone, they have a special importance for girls, since many girls are socialized to put other people's needs first. "For the most part of my life, I've been a people pleaser," explains a young woman named Cassie. "I would pay special attention to the positive feedback I received for being 'nice' and pleasing others and I derived almost all of my self-worth from putting the feelings and needs of other people well above my own."[20] In the #MeToo era, these attitudes are changing. Young women are learning that there is nothing wrong with being outspoken about their needs, including their boundaries.

> "Setting boundaries allows teens to communicate with other people about what is OK and what is not OK with them and is essential for teen friendships and dating relationships."[19]
>
> —Sherri Gordon, bullying prevention advocate

Relationship boundaries can be sorted into two general categories. Physical boundaries are limits that people set on how and when they choose to be touched and on their physical space. Emotional boundaries are limits people set on how they want to be treated.

Physical Boundaries

No one ever has the right to touch others who do not want to be touched or to touch them in a way they do not want to be touched. This is a general rule that applies to all relationships, not just romantic ones. It is *always* okay to say no to physical touch, and it is very important to respect other people's physical boundaries.

Some of the hardest boundaries to enforce involve touch that may seem to others to be no big deal. It can feel uncomfortable to say no to a hug or a high five from a friend. In dating relationships, holding hands and snuggling might seem like no big deal. However, if someone does not want to hold hands or snuggle, that is unwanted touch, and people need to respect that.

Physical boundaries often relate to physical space. When two people are having a conversation, they instinctively place an invisible boundary between themselves. Crossing the boundary—or standing too close to the other person—can feel invasive. In a dating relationship, if one person sits too closely to someone who does not want this, that is an infringement of a physical boundary.

In all relationships, boundaries are important because they help keep people comfortable and safe. This is important in dating relationships, which come with emotional risks like heartbreak and physical risks like sexual assault.

Physical and sexual boundaries in dating relationships are more complicated than boundaries in other relationships, but the same basic guidelines apply. Do not touch someone who does not want to be touched or touch someone in a way he or she does not want to be touched, *no matter what*. Remember, when it comes to sex and other physical intimacy, failure to respect boundaries is sexual assault.

Physical violence, like hitting someone, also falls into the category of violating a physical boundary. Physical violence is never acceptable in a relationship of any kind and should always be considered out-of-bounds and grounds for immediately ending a relationship.

Emotional Boundaries

If physical boundaries are limits that people set about how they want to be touched, emotional boundaries are limits that people set about how they want to be treated. The Love Is Respect organization explains it like this: "Emotional boundaries are limitations surrounding your feelings, vulnerability, and trust. These boundaries help you determine how much of your heart you want to share with your partner."[21]

Emotional boundaries often involve how partners talk to one another. For example, some people enjoy being teased, but others do not. If someone tells their boyfriend that they do not want to be teased—or says they are okay with being teased about some things but not others—they are setting an emotional boundary.

Emotional boundaries are also about levels of emotional closeness. Some people are uncomfortable sharing personal information and talking about their emotions. Other people may be uncomfortable sharing information about certain topics. Just as no one should feel pressured to be sexually intimate in ways they do not want, no one should feel pressured to be emotionally intimate.

> "Emotional boundaries are limitations surrounding your feelings, vulnerability, and trust. These boundaries help you determine how much of your heart you want to share with your partner."[21]
>
> —Love Is Respect, a project of the National Domestic Violence Hotline

In dating relationships, time boundaries are important and can become contentious. Many young people are very busy with school, activities, friends, work, and more and do not have unlimited time to put into a relationship. If a partner does not respect someone's need to spend his or her time doing other things, this may be a red flag that the relationship is unhealthy.

How to Set Boundaries

There are three steps to setting boundaries: defining boundaries, communicating boundaries, and enforcing boundaries. These are all skills that take practice, especially in dating relationships.

The first step to establishing boundaries in relationships is figuring out what they are—which may sound obvious, but this is not something people commonly think about. Before individuals begin a relationship, it can be useful to take a mental inventory of the things that are important to them. What are their values,

Boundaries: Red, Yellow, or Green?

As the COVID-19 pandemic waned and people started going back to school and work, people started having new conversations about boundaries. Some people did not want to hug or shake hands, especially because the virus was still around. Other people were excited about being in close proximity to other people after the long period of social isolation. To address this issue, some schools and companies started using variations of a red, yellow, or green system. Students or employees chose to wear red, yellow, or green wristbands or stickers. People who chose red wristbands wanted no contact; yellow meant limited contact, like fist bumps or high fives; green meant hugs were welcome. The red, yellow, or green system is an explicit way to communicate boundaries—and people can do similar things when it comes to setting boundaries about physical relationships. For example, writer Rachel Kramer Bussel suggests that partners create a Yes, No, Maybe chart to signify sexual activities that each partner would like to do, never do, or possibly try.

religious or otherwise? What goals and time constraints are they not willing to sacrifice for a relationship? How do they expect to be treated? What limits do they want to set on sexual behavior? These are all useful things to think about ahead of time, since it is harder to think about boundaries in the moment—especially sexual boundaries.

When it comes to boundaries, everyone has deal breakers. Deal breakers are nonnegotiable boundaries that someone feels too strongly about to change his or her mind. Deal breakers might be "no sex without a condom," or "no kissing other people." Some deal breakers reflect religious beliefs or other moral codes; for example, an observant Jewish person might refuse to go on dates on Friday nights because of the Sabbath. If a boundary is important enough to be a deal breaker, that means it is not up for negotiation. Following the boundary is a prerequisite for being in the relationship. Of course, any kind of physical or sexual violence in a relationship is a deal breaker.

Secondary boundaries are also important and need to be respected. These are boundaries that might change in the future. For example, someone might decide that "no sex" is a boundary but feel there is a possibility of changing this in a year or two. Secondary boundaries might be more fluid; for example, "no going out on dates on school nights" might have some exceptions—like a big concert, for instance.

After choosing boundaries, the next step is to decide exactly where the boundary lines lie. What behaviors are outside the boundary—and therefore unacceptable—and what behaviors are acceptable because they are within the boundary? Where should lines be drawn when it comes to sexual activity?

One important thing to remember about boundaries is that they can be changed. If someone decides that something is okay—partial nudity, for example—but it feels wrong in the moment, he or she has every right to say no. Boundaries are not contracts that give the other person the absolute right to do whatever was agreed upon initially. Boundaries are designed to protect people emotionally and physically—and if they are not working, they can be modified.

Before individuals begin a relationship, it can be useful to take a mental inventory of the things that are important to them. They should consider their values, goals, and how they want to be treated.

Healthy Boundaries Versus Manipulative Rules

Healthy boundaries allow people to protect themselves emotionally and physically. They are not created with the intent to hurt or control another person, even if that person does not like the boundary. Sometimes people call something a boundary when in fact it is not—it is a rule created for the primary purpose of controlling someone else's behavior. For example, imagine that a girl tells her boyfriend that he is not allowed to be friends with other girls, under any circumstances. When he gets upset, she informs him that this is a boundary for her and that he has to respect it. This may sound like a boundary, but the main purpose of it is not to protect herself emotionally—it is a rule designed to control her boyfriend's behavior, and it is completely unreasonable. As advice columnist Carolyn Hax explains, "Our boundaries apply inward, to ourselves; rules apply outward, to others. . . . [That is] a common, self-serving misinterpretation of what a boundary is—mistaking 'what I want' for 'what you have to do.'" Healthy boundaries do not require other people to do things that are unfair or unreasonable or that violate their own boundaries.

Carolyn Hax, "Wife's 'Boundaries' with Teen Son Feel Controlling," *Washington Post*, December 2, 2022. www.washingtonpost.com.

Communicating Boundaries

After someone defines what their boundaries are, he or she needs to communicate this to the other person. If possible, these are good discussions to have at a neutral time—like during lunch or at a coffee shop—before the issue in question comes up. Talking about boundaries in person is ideal, but if this is too intimidating, other communication methods will do—like a video call, a text, or a handwritten note. If necessary, communicating a boundary in the moment is fine too—and is definitely better than not communicating it at all.

Boundaries need to be communicated clearly and unambiguously. For example, if a boy does not want to have sex until after high school, and this is a deal breaker for him, he should state this clearly and not hint at it. People should never assume that others can guess what their boundaries are, and hinting about boundaries is an invitation for misinterpretation. It might feel uncomfortable or rude to talk about what someone wants directly, but this is very important. Everyone deserves to have their boundaries respected fully, and this will not happen without clear communication.

Setting boundaries in a relationship is not a one-time thing. Throughout a relationship, people may need to discuss new boundaries as the need arises. For example, if a girl's boyfriend keeps showing up at her workplace uninvited, she needs to tell him that work is off-limits. In addition, established boundaries may need to be revisited. If a couple are about to graduate and go to different colleges, they may decide to revisit their agreement not to date other people.

Is it important to be nice when setting boundaries? In most cases this is preferable—but it is important to remember that there is nothing inherently unkind about setting boundaries. If people are too worried about being nice, they might not get their point across. However, boundaries can be set kindly. As psychotherapist Sharon Martin explains, boundary setting is both kind and more effective when the focus is on the needs of the person setting the boundary, as opposed to the other person's behavior. "Setting a boundary is about communicating what you need and expect," says Martin. "In the process, it may be important to gently call out someone's hurtful behavior, but that shouldn't be the focus. Focusing on what someone has done wrong is likely to make them defensive. Instead, lead with how you feel and what you need."[22]

Remember, though, that relationships are not one-sided. Both partners need to be willing to respect each other's boundaries. In fact, since setting boundaries can be intimidating, it can be helpful to encourage the other person to share his or hers—and if the other person's boundaries are ever unclear, ask. In healthy relationships, everyone communicates openly about their boundaries, and everybody listens.

> "Setting a boundary is about communicating what you need and expect. In the process, it may be important to gently call out someone's hurtful behavior, but that shouldn't be the focus. . . . Instead, lead with how you feel and what you need."[22]
>
> —Sharon Martin, psychotherapist

Enforcing Boundaries

The hardest part about boundaries is this: people do not like them. Boundaries interfere with what another person wants—whether that's sex, attention, or something else. To enforce boundaries, people may need to let others know—often at awkward moments—that they *really* mean it. Expect pushback, and be ready for it.

There are a number of different kinds of pushback. To illustrate, here's an example: imagine that a girl is having a party, and her boyfriend wants to bring alcohol. She sets a boundary by telling him no. This is a deal breaker for her because she does not want to violate her parents' trust. Hopefully, he will accept this and move on, but if not, he might push back and try to get his way.

When someone pushes back against a boundary, a good place to begin is by restating or clarifying it. The girl can restate her boundary to show she is serious—no alcohol at the party, period. If appropriate, it can be helpful to make a statement that validates the other person's position without giving in. In this case she might tell her boyfriend she understands where he is coming from—he wants their friends to have a great time at the party, and she wants this too. However, they will have to have a good time without alcohol.

Boundary-Pushing Strategies

One common strategy that boundary pushers employ is negotiation, or trying to move the line. The boyfriend might try to move the line and ask if he can bring beer to the party, but no other alcohol. If she says yes, she has moved the line. Now that her boyfriend knows that the line can be moved, he might push it further and try to bring other kinds of alcohol. If someone succeeds in moving the line past an established boundary, he or she may do so continually—which is something that can happen in sexual relationships.

Another common boundary-pushing tactic is to try to wear someone down with a lengthy argument, until they lose the argu-

Setting boundaries in a relationship can be difficult. When enforcing boundaries, be ready for pushback.

ment or give up. If the boyfriend tries this, she should disengage from the argument. "Avoid arguing with a boundary pusher, since it's a slippery slope to giving in," explains psychology professor Shawn M. Burn. "If they start to argue or persist, shut it down by saying something like, 'I know this isn't what you wanted to hear, but my mind is made up.'"[23]

Some boundary pushers try to break a boundary by trivializing it. The boyfriend might tell the girl that she is making a big deal over nothing. After all, a few beers are no big deal, right? This is another good situation for disengagement. She could get into a lengthy argument about why a few beers *are* a big deal—or she can just tell him that it is a big deal to her and the matter is closed.

Some pushback tactics are so emotionally manipulative that the best thing to do is end the conversation—and in some cases end the relationship. One manipulative tactic is to belittle or mock someone—like if the boyfriend says that people will only come if there is alcohol because no one likes her. Another manipulative technique is to issue a threat—like threatening to break up with her if she does not allow alcohol. He also might ignore her boundary altogether and show up at the party with alcohol anyway. These tactics are red flags that a relationship is unhealthy and quite possibly needs to end.

It's important to know that if a person does not like a boundary, he or she always has the option to leave. Someone can enforce a boundary as a condition of the relationship—but that means that sometimes, a partner might opt out of the relationship. Sometimes this speaks badly about the partner—like a guy who wants to break up because he can't bring alcohol to a party—but sometimes people just have different needs. For example, if one person in a relationship only has time to date once a week, and the other person wants to spend more time together, this couple may not be compatible.

Remember, there is nothing selfish or unkind about putting one's needs first and setting boundaries. Everyone deserves to have emotional and physical boundaries, and no one has to be liked at any cost. Nor is it necessary to maintain relationships at any cost. Breakups can be hard—really hard—but ultimately, dating a boundary pusher is worse. As the organization Love Is Respect, a project of the National Domestic Violence Hotline, says: "If your partner tries to minimize your needs or violates the boundaries you established, then they aren't showing you the respect and trustworthiness you deserve."[24]

CHAPTER THREE

Consent in the #MeToo Era

In conversations about consent, people often bring up the phrase "no means no." This is a very important concept. When someone says no to sex—or to anything else—that must be respected. No does not mean maybe. No is not an invitation to talk someone into yes. No means no, period. Anyone who does not take no for an answer is violating his or her partner's boundaries in the most serious way.

However, when it comes to consent in the #MeToo era, no means no is just the starting point. Sometimes people say yes to sexual activity for a number of unhealthy reasons, like coercion, pressure, or fear or because they are under the influence of alcohol or drugs. Just because someone does not say no does not necessarily mean they are saying yes. Yael, a college freshman, writes about a sexual experience that she regretted. "I was so embarrassed," she says. "There I was: a little freshman, naked in a senior's bed. I was so ashamed to have put myself in that situation that I felt as if I had to go through with it. So I did. It was physically painful in the moment and emotionally painful the following days and weeks."[25]

In this case, Yael did not say no. However, she also did not enthusiastically and unambiguously say yes—and the reality is, she had sex that she very much did not want. While the senior in this story did not assault Yael, he also did not make sure she really wanted to be there.

> "Enthusiastic consent is a newer model for understanding consent that focuses on a positive expression of consent. Simply put, enthusiastic consent means looking for the presence of a 'yes' rather than the absence of a 'no.'"[26]
>
> —Rape, Abuse & Incest National Network

In the #MeToo era, consent is about making sure each partner in a sexual encounter absolutely wants it to happen. Sometimes this is called enthusiastic consent or affirmative consent. As the RAINN website explains, "Enthusiastic consent is a newer model for understanding consent that focuses on a positive expression of consent. Simply put, enthusiastic consent means looking for the presence of a 'yes' rather than the absence of a 'no.'"[26]

Intimate physical experiences should not be upsetting. They should be fun and safe, and this can only happen if both partners are both genuinely enthusiastic about them. This goes for all kinds of physical experiences—kissing, intercourse, or anything else. Healthy, respectful consent happens when two people both say yes in a manner that is fully informed, free of coercion, specific, reversable, and enthusiastic.

Consent Should be Fully Informed

Informed consent means a person has access to all the information he or she needs to make a consensual decision about sexual activity. This is more than just a personal issue. There are laws about informed consent, which vary by state. If a person is not fully able to understand the act to which he or she is consenting, then the person does not have the legal capacity to consent. This includes some people with brain injuries or developmental disabilities. It also includes people who are too drunk or too high to fully understand their actions, as well as people who are unconscious or asleep.

The legal capacity to consent also relates to age. In some cases people under age eighteen are not legally able to give consent to intercourse and other sexual activities, even if they want to. The laws about this also vary by state. For example, in Colorado the age of consent is seventeen, which means that it is not a crime to have sex with a seventeen-year-old who gives consent. Colorado teenagers who are fifteen and sixteen can legally consent to sex unless the other person is ten or more years older than them. Sex with a person who is legally unable to consent because of his or her age is called statutory rape, which is a crime often punishable by jail time.

Informed consent goes beyond the legal capacity to consent. Anything that interferes with a person's ability to make informed decisions about sexual activity is a problem. If a person lies or withholds information in order to get a partner to have sex, this violates the principle of informed consent. This includes lying about condom use, lying about being single, or withholding information about a sexually transmitted disease (STD). In addition, just because state law says that someone is legally sober enough to consent to sex does not always mean they are truly sober enough to consent in a fully informed way. If there is the slightest doubt about whether someone is too drunk or high to make an informed decision, always err on the side of stopping.

In the #MeToo era, consent is about making sure each partner in a sexual encounter absolutely wants it to happen. Sometimes this is called enthusiastic consent or affirmative consent.

Consent Should be Free from Coercion

In addition to being fully informed, consent should be free of coercion. Coercion is pushing someone to say yes when he or she really wants to say no. It is not okay to be physical with someone who has been coerced into saying yes.

> "I am surprised at how much sex I have had in my life that I didn't want to have. I said yes because it was too much trouble to say no. I said yes because I didn't want to have to defend my 'no.'"[27]
>
> —Margaret Cho, comedian

One common coercive tactic is to turn the discussion into a debate (a tactic also commonly used for pushing boundaries). This includes badgering someone until the person feels like it is easier just to give in. It also includes presenting a long list of reasons for why the person should say yes. This puts the onus on that person to argue against each reason. "I am surprised at how much sex I have had in my life that I didn't want to have," explains comedian Margaret Cho. "I said yes because it was too much trouble to say no. I said yes because I didn't want to have to defend my 'no.'"[27]

It is inappropriate to debate with someone about whether he or she has a legitimate reason to say no. No one should ever have to justify saying no, and no one ever owes anyone else sex.

Emotional Coercion

Another common tactic is emotional coercion, which is when someone manipulates someone else's feelings to get what he or she wants. Guilt is a popular form of this. Isabella talks about how when she was fourteen, she was emotionally coerced by her older girlfriend Rachel. "The first time we kissed was the first day we started going out," says Isabella. "I was not ready, but she told me we needed to make our relationship official. When I told her I wasn't ready [to have sex] she asked me, 'Well don't you love me?' I said, 'Yes of course,' but she wanted me to prove it."[28]

Emotional coercion can also come in the form of belittling. Telling someone that he or she is an immature baby for saying no

Comedian Margaret Cho (pictured) suggests women often agree to sex not because they want to, but because it is too difficult and too much trouble to refuse.

is emotional coercion. So is telling someone that he or she has to say yes because no one else will ever find him or her attractive.

Another coercive tactic is the use of threats and punishment. Threatening to break up with someone if he or she says no is emotional coercion. So is punishing someone with anger or a bad mood, or withholding attention or affection. Other threats might include refusing to take someone to an event like a prom or threatening to share sexually explicit photos or otherwise damage someone's reputation. In some cases coercion can also be physical—as in threatening physical harm to someone if he or she does not say yes.

Coercion can also be achieved by offering someone an incentive if he or she says yes. An example of this is agreeing to date someone or offering to take someone to the prom only if he or she says yes to sex.

Emotional coercion can be especially damaging if one person in the relationship is vulnerable in some way. This can happen if someone in the relationship has low self-esteem. It can also happen if one person in the relationship has more power in some way. Perhaps this person is older or perceived as being more popular, or perhaps he or she is in a position of authority, like the other person's work supervisor or coach. The stronger person can emotionally coerce the weaker one by claiming the person has to say yes to prove his or her worth.

It can be challenging to stand up to emotional coercion, but it is important to do so. No one deserves to be pressured into sexual activity that they do not want.

Consent Should Be Specific and Reversable

Consent is not a ticket to an all-you-can-eat buffet. At a buffet customers pay one price, and then they can take as much as they want of anything in the restaurant. Consent does not work like that. If someone consents to something once, their partner does not

The History of No Means No

The phrase "no means no" became popular on college campuses in the 1980s in response to older, misogynistic attitudes about consent. In generations past, many boys (who were assumed to be heterosexual) were taught to see sex with girls as a conquest to prove their masculinity. Boys were taught that no was an obstacle, not an answer. They were also taught that when a girl says no, she does not necessarily mean no, so it was okay to pressure her to go further. In addition, they were told that certain kinds of behavior implied yes, even if a girl was saying no—like if a girl wore revealing clothing, flirted with a boy at a party, or had a reputation for being promiscuous. No means no calls this all into question. If a person says no, then the answer is no, no matter what.

then have the freedom to do anything he or she wants, as many times as he or she wants. Consent is specific—it is permission to do one thing, one time. This does not mean that partners need to ask permission for every small touch or action. However, it does mean that if someone wants to do something more intimate than what the couple are currently doing (like taking off each other's shirts for the first time), they need to get consent.

> "You get the final say over what happens with your body. It doesn't matter if you hooked up before or even if you said yes earlier and you changed your mind. You're allowed to say 'stop' at any time, and your partner needs to respect that."[29]
>
> —Planned Parenthood

Consent is also reversable. Anyone can give consent to something and then change his or her mind—and there is nothing wrong with that. "You get the final say over what happens with your body," explains Planned Parenthood's website. "It doesn't matter if you hooked up before or even if you said yes earlier and you changed your mind. You're allowed to say 'stop' at any time, and your partner needs to respect that."[29]

Saying no after saying yes can feel awkward, especially in the moment—and girls might feel like they cannot change their mind because of gender roles. However, author and activist Emily Linden writes:

> You might feel pressure not to disappoint them. As women, we are taught to put others' feelings above our own comfort, so we might find ourselves considering having sex with someone rather than risk offending them. Just to be polite! But you are perfectly entitled to change your mind, even if you're not quite sure why, even if you made a promise, even if you've had sex with this person before.[30]

Consent Should Be Enthusiastic

There are two important requirements for sexual activity that may seem obvious—and yet these requirements are often ignored. First, one partner really wants to do it—and second, the other partner really wants to do it too. "Enthusiastic consent is not coerced, pressured, or forced in any way," says sex educator Gigi Engle. "It's when you're super down to clown, and everyone is extremely excited about it."[31]

Unfortunately, there are a lot of unenthusiastic reasons why people say yes to sexual activity. They feel lonely or bored. They want to make their partner happy. They feel obligated. They feel unattractive and want to prove to themselves otherwise. They are worried about being dumped. They don't want to be the only virgin in their friend group. They do not have a good reason to say no, so they might as well get it over with. Sexual activity under these circumstances is not fun, and it is not healthy.

People also sometimes say yes to sexual activity when they feel ambivalent about it. Maybe they are not sure. Maybe they are very nervous. Maybe they kind of want to do it, maybe? Ambivalence is not enthusiasm, and enthusiasm should be a clear, unambiguous, happy yes. If both partners do not feel enthusiastic about sexual activity, there is no reason to continue.

Communicating Consent

In practice, how do partners communicate consent to one another? This may seem complicated, and on the one hand, it is. Learning how to communicate about consent is a skill that needs to be practiced—just like learning how to set boundaries. On the other hand, the basic premise of communicating about consent is simple. Each partner should communicate what he or she wants and does not want and should respect the other partner's wishes.

For starters, never forget that no means no. In the #MeToo era, no means no is just the starting place for understanding consent—but it is an important starting place. If someone does not want to do something, that person should say no, and his or her partner needs to respect this. Pushing back against no is the opposite of enthusiastic consent, and forcing someone to do something when he or she has said no is sexual assault.

So if nobody says no, then what? The next step is to make sure that everything that happens is done with enthusiastic

Saying no after saying yes can feel awkward and girls might feel like they cannot change their mind because of gender roles. But consent is always reversable.

consent—in other words, that yes *really* means yes. This means that clear, unambiguous communication is important, and the best way to do this is through explicit verbal consent. "It's simple," explains Planned Parenthood's website. "Ask: 'Can I [fill in the blank]?' or 'Do you want me to do [fill in the blank]?' And listen for the answer."[32]

Since people sometimes feel pressured to say yes, it is important to verify that yes is enthusiastic. One way to do this is to pay attention to tone. When someone says yes, does that person sound enthusiastic, or does he or she sound hesitant or unsure? It is also important to observe a partner's nonverbal cues. Do his or her nonverbal actions seem positive—like eye contact, smiling, or nodding—or does the person's body language indicate that he or she is not fully comfortable?

If someone's yes seems shaky, make sure he or she understands that no is an acceptable answer—and that there will be no negative consequences for saying no. Planned Parenthood recommends using check-in phrases like, "I want to make sure you want to do this. Should I keep going?" and "It's okay if you're not into this. We can do something else. What do you think?"[33] Keep in mind that silence does not mean yes; actual verbal confirmations are crucial, since silence can be easily misinterpreted.

Do people need to get consent for everything? For relationships in early stages, yes, although this does not mean that every small touch needs a request for consent. However, moving up a level (like from touching someone's back to touching their genitals) requires consent. When couples have been together for a while, sometimes it is less necessary to ask directly for consent. Couples can agree to blanket consent, which means they agree that they can proceed without explicit permission—but still need to stop if someone says no. Still, even with blanket consent, it is important that both partners pay attention to nonverbal cues and check in to make sure there is enthusiastic consent.

Colleges and Affirmative Consent

In 1991 Antioch University (now Antioch College) made headlines with its groundbreaking Sexual Offense Prevention Policy. This was inspired by a group of students who thought there was not enough being done to prevent sexual assault on campus. The policy was based on the concept of affirmative consent, defined as "the act of willingly and verbally agreeing to engage in specific sexual conduct" which must be "obtained each and every time there is sexual activity." The policy, which still exists today, says that the person who initiates sexual activity is responsible for getting verbal consent for every new level of sexual activity. At the time, the policy received a good deal of negative publicity by those who felt the school was going overboard by legislating verbal consent. However, today many schools have similar policies. In fact, in 2014 California adopted the "affirmative consent" law, which mandates affirmative consent at California colleges and universities.

Antioch College. "Sexual Offense Prevention Policy (SOPP) & Title IX," 2022. www.antiochcollege.com

Open Communication

Is asking for consent awkward? Maybe at times—but the reward for this is that both partners feel safe and comfortable, and no one does something he or she doesn't really want to do. Molly, a college student, explains how much she appreciated a partner who asked for consent:

> He had asked if he could kiss me. Instead of a moist darting tongue, I received a question. Whenever we spooned, he would ask if he could touch me. A marvel. It was such a simple question, yet I had never heard it. I was accustomed to my partners groping my breasts or my butt while I attempted to fall asleep. I never felt more like an object than when their arousal didn't even require my consciousness. Hearing this simple question—"Can I touch you?"—reminded me I should feel like a person.[34]

In healthy relationships, no one should ever do something sexually unless he or she genuinely wants to. Open communication about consent is important to make sure both partners feel safe, happy, and free to control what happens to their own bodies.

CHAPTER FOUR

Boundaries and Consent: How to Support Others

The #MeToo era represents a cultural shift in how people talk about boundaries and consent. However, older attitudes have not disappeared. The #MeToo tweets showed that sexual assault and harassment are commonplace. When it comes to creating a world where respecting boundaries and consent is universally valued, there is a long way to go. So how can this be changed?

One of the most important things everyone can do is to show solidarity with people who have experienced sexual assault or harassment or whose boundaries have otherwise been challenged or broken. People show solidarity by standing together with survivors, believing them, and making them feel seen and heard. They also show solidarity by taking action—both by helping individuals who have been hurt and by working to make broader changes in communities and in society as a whole.

People can be supportive of survivors regardless of whether they have experienced sexual assault or harassment in similar ways. Those who have had similar experiences can offer support by discussing their own experiences. That was a big part of what the #MeToo tweets were about—people with similar experiences standing together and telling each other that they were not alone.

One specific form of solidarity is called allyship. An ally is someone who stands in solidarity with people from a community that has been discriminated against and treated unjustly. For example, White people can strive to be allies to people of color, and heterosexual people can strive to be allies to LGBTQ people. During the #MeToo tweets, many men expressed their horror about what women revealed about their experiences and declared themselves to be allies. Allies have to be careful not to speak for people in the marginalized group; instead, they should listen to what people have to say about their own lived experiences. However, sometimes allies can use their privileged position in ways to help marginalized groups.

Change happens when people stand together and take action. Here are some ways to support survivors and work toward change in society as a whole.

Believe Victims

One of the most powerful things supporters can do to help sexual assault victims is simply to believe them and to make sure they know that they are believed. Years after she was sexually assaulted as a teenager, actress Sarah Hyland from *Modern Family* wrote about why she kept silent about the attack. "He was a friend," she wrote. "It was New Year's Eve my senior year of high school. Everyone was drunk. He broke in to the bathroom I was in. I hoped it was a dream but my ripped tights in the morning proved otherwise. I thought no one would believe me. I didn't want to be called dramatic. After all I didn't say no."[35]

One reason why Hyland did not report her attack is that she feared that people would not believe her. Unfortunately, this is common—and one of the main reasons why the vast majority of sexual assaults are not reported. "Fear of retaliation, guilt, regret, humiliation—there are a number of reasons women don't come forward about sexual assault, but it's the fear that they won't be believed—or that they'll even be blamed—that often prevails,"[36] explains Laura Palumbo of the National Sexual Violence Resource Center.

It is good to show solidarity with people who have experienced sexual assault or harassment. People show solidarity by standing together with survivors and making them feel like they are seen and heard.

Despite widespread fear by survivors that they will not be believed, very few accusations of sexual assault are false. If someone says they have been sexually assaulted, then statistically speaking, they are almost certainly telling the truth. Many studies show that only about 5 percent of sexual assault accusations are false—and according to sociologist Joanne Belknap, even that low estimate is inaccurately high. For one thing, this includes many reported incidents that were declared false by police officers without a trial or a thorough investigation. Moreover, argues Belknap, since the majority of sexual assault cases are not reported, especially on college campuses, this means the percentage of total sexual assaults that are reported falsely is probably less than 1 percent.

Do Not Blame the Victim

Another reason that Hyland did not report her rape was because at the time, she felt like she was partially to blame for it—and she feared that others would blame her too. She blamed herself because she was drunk and because she did not say no.

Hyland's fear that she would be blamed may not have been unfounded. Blaming or partially blaming sexual assault victims is very common—which is a major reason why so many victims have internalized these assumptions and believe themselves to be at fault. Blame sometimes comes from people in the victim's life, and sometimes it comes from law enforcement. "While victims of other violent crimes usually do not have to explain what they 'did' to become victimized, victims of sexual violence are all too often forced to defend their actions leading up to an experience of sexual violence," explains the Maryland Coalition Against Sexual Assault. "This contributes to [a] difficult environment for survivors to share their stories when they are blamed, disbelieved, and shamed."[37]

If someone says that he or she has been sexually assaulted, do not blame the person in any way, and assure the person that he or she is not to blame, no matter what. Lori Bednarchik, a health education specialist, says:

> "While victims of other violent crimes usually do not have to explain what they 'did' to become victimized, victims of sexual violence are all too often forced to defend their actions leading up to an experience of sexual violence."[37]
>
> —Maryland Coalition Against Sexual Assault

> Nobody deserves to be sexually assaulted/raped or abused . . . no matter what they were wearing, how much they drank, how they were dancing, even if they were flirting or went to his/her room with them, if they had a previous romantic or sexual relationship, how late they stayed out, who they got a ride from, etc. etc. etc. Being sexually assaulted, raped, or abused is never the victim's fault.[38]

Sexual assaulters are fully cognizant human beings who made an active decision to harm someone, and they are fully responsible for that action.

What Does It Mean to Be an Active Listener?

Supporters can help survivors by listening—and, in particular, by being active listeners. "Active listening is a communication skill that involves going beyond simply hearing the words that another person speaks, but also seeking to understand the meaning and intent behind them," explains therapist Arlin Cuncic. "It requires being an active participant in the communication process." When individuals listen actively, they offer their full attention and demonstrate interest with eye contact, nodding, and other nonverbal cues. They try not to let their mind wander—and they put away their cell phone. When listening, concentrate on what is being said, without trying to think of what to say next. Let the speaker dominate the conversation without interruption. Be patient with long silences; these are times for the speaker to gather his or her thoughts. Invite the speaker to say more (if he or she wants) with open-ended questions like, "Can you tell me more about that?"

Arlin Cuncic, "What Is Active Listening?" Verywell Mind, November 9, 2022. www.verywellmind.com.

Showing Solidarity by Listening

When individuals talk about a traumatic experience, including sexual assault, supporters may worry about saying the wrong thing to them. These are difficult conversations to have, and there is no one-size-fits-all method for responding to a sexual assault survivor. One thing that supporters can always do is tell the survivor that they are very sorry this happened and offer to help in any way that the survivor needs. Here are some other important things to keep in mind.

First, if the survivor wants to talk about what happened, the supporter can help by just listening. For many sexual assault victims, feeling heard can be very therapeutic. The Penn State Student Affairs website sums it up like this: "It takes incredible strength and courage for someone to disclose that they are a victim or survivor. Listen actively and without judgment. Avoid asking questions or digging for details. It's best to allow them to control what information they share."[39] Supporters should strive for what is known as active listening. Active listening means concentrating fully on what is being said and allowing the speaker to express himself or herself without judgment and without interruption.

However, not all survivors want to talk about what happened, or if they do, they do not want to talk about all the details. This is a boundary that needs to be respected. "Many rape victims don't want to re-live or re-state all the details of what happened," explains Susan Storm, a sexual assault survivor. "Some may want to talk about it to find healing or support; that's fine. Just don't ask them for details, let them be the ones to share them."[40] Supporters can help by offering to listen to the survivor again at a later time, if or when the survivor wants this.

When a supporter who is listening actively has had a similar experience, he or she may wonder if it is appropriate or helpful to share that experience. This depends. On the one hand, a supporter's main goal in this situation is to listen actively and not interrupt. The survivor needs to be the focus of the conversation. On the other hand, if a supporter has had a similar experience, it might be helpful to share it as a way to let the survivor know

If a sexual assault survivor wants to talk about what happened, a supporter can help by just listening. For many sexual assault victims, feeling heard can be very therapeutic.

he or she is not alone. After all, this is what happened during #MeToo—survivors empowered each other by sharing similar experiences. Survivors should use their judgment on whether to share—and should never feel obligated to share their experiences or all of the details.

Avoid Minimizing the Survivor's Experience

One thing supporters need to do is avoid minimizing the experience of the survivor. Sometimes people try to minimize things to help another person see the bigger picture and feel better; for example, someone might tell a friend that the D he got on a test is not a big deal because there is plenty of time to pull up his grade. But when it comes to talking to a survivor, this is *not* the time to tell someone to see the big picture—what happened *was* a big deal. Never, ever tell someone in this situation to get over it—this is one of the most dismissive things someone can say and a good way to lose a friend.

Another way that people minimize a survivor's experience is by saying he or she should feel relieved the experience was not worse. Storm cautions, "Don't say something like, 'Well, at least you weren't like that girl I read about in the news who was locked in a basement,' or 'well, at least you weren't raped by someone you really trusted.' Making statements like this is dehumanizing to the survivor, and belittles their pain."[41]

In addition to not minimizing the survivor's experience, it is also important to not trivialize the courage it takes for the survivor to come forward. Gossiping about someone else's sexual assault is a terrible violation of trust. Doing so trivializes what the victim has experienced and the courage it took to speak up. Supporters absolutely need to respect a victim's privacy.

> "Don't say something like, 'Well, at least you weren't like that girl I read about in the news who was locked in a basement,' or 'well, at least you weren't raped by someone you really trusted.' Making statements like this is dehumanizing to the survivor, and belittles their pain."[41]
>
> —Susan Storm, sexual assault survivor

How to Help Someone Who Has Just Been Assaulted

If someone has just been assaulted, the first thing to do is make sure the person is physically safe from the attacker. If not, or if the person is badly injured, call 911. Assure the survivor that what happened was not his or her fault and that he or she is not alone. Encourage the person to go to an emergency room or urgent care facility and help him or her get there if possible. The medical professionals will treat any injuries; they may also test for STDs, administer medication to prevent the human immunodeficiency virus, and offer emergency contraception to prevent pregnancy. They may also administer a rape kit, which is an exam designed to collect physical evidence of a rape. (For this reason, rape victims should not shower or clean up before the exam—which may be very disconcerting for a victim, but it's important.) In most states, teenagers can get treatment for sexual assault and report the crime without parental involvement. The victim can then report the crime to law enforcement, if this is what he or she chooses. Not all sexual assault victims want this, so respect the person's wishes.

Helping Survivors Find Resources

Supporters are not expected to have all the answers. In addition to listening, supporters can help by referring the survivor to someone who is professionally trained to work with sexual abuse survivors, like a school counselor or social worker. Many communities have crisis centers and hotlines to help survivors, and so do college campuses.

Sometimes referring a survivor to someone else is important because it may be too difficult for the supporter to listen. Hearing someone talk about a traumatic experience can be very difficult—and possibly even retraumatizing if the supporter has gone through something similar. If a conversation is retraumatizing or otherwise feels like too much, a supporter should not feel guilty about ending it. In this case a supporter can help by recommending that the survivor speak with someone with professional expertise.

It is up to survivors whether they want to talk to someone else about their experiences. Part of respecting privacy is not seeking additional help for the survivor without permission. However, there are two big exceptions to this: if a survivor is in danger of being assaulted again by the assailant, or if a survivor is talking about self-harm or suicide. If this is the case, the supporter should speak as soon as possible to a trusted adult who has the power to help—like a school counselor, a social worker, a parent, or a religious leader like a youth pastor.

Taking Action

Supporters can do more than just listen—they can be active bystanders. According to the Rape, Abuse & Incest National Network, "An active bystander is someone who interrupts a potentially harmful situation, especially when it comes to sexual violence. They may not be directly involved but they do have the choice and opportunity to speak up and intervene."[42] While anyone can be an active bystander, sometimes this is one way that boys can use their position of privilege to be an ally to a girl.

There are three Ds when it comes to being an active bystander: direct, delegate, and distract. A direct approach is when a supporter takes immediate action to intervene in a dangerous or disturbing situation. For example, if a supporter sees boys harassing a girl in the hallway and trying to touch her, the supporter could demand that they stop and then walk the girl to class. To delegate means to get others involved. For example, if a supporter sees a guy at a party pressuring a drunk girl for sex, the supporter can ask the girl's friends to take her home. To distract means to disrupt a dangerous situation to help someone get out of it. For example, to help the drunk girl at the party, the supporter might tell the guy that his car is being towed so the girl can get away and leave with her friends.

One situation in which an active bystander can help is street harassment. Women and girls live in a world where it is common

> "An active bystander is someone who interrupts a potentially harmful situation, especially when it comes to sexual violence. They may not be directly involved but they do have the choice and opportunity to speak up and intervene."[42]
>
> —Rape, Abuse & Incest National Network

Women live in a world where it is common for men to shout sexual things at them in public places. An active bystander can help stop this everyday harassment by standing up to it.

for boys and men to shout out sexual things at them in public places and to demand attention from them in places like public transportation. By standing up to street harassment, an active bystander sends a message to other people that this kind of harassment is not acceptable. Supporters can tell boys in school to stop harassing girls and report them to a teacher if they do not. If it is safe, they can also tell men in public to stop or report the harassment to law enforcement. Again, this is a situation in which boys and men can be allies to girls and women, since it may be safer for a boy to intervene in a public situation like this than a girl.

Speaking Out

Being an active bystander is more than just taking immediate action to help individuals. Supporters can also be active bystanders by speaking out against everyday things that normalize sexual assault and other boundary violations. For example, if a supporter hears someone telling a rape joke, he or she can say that it's not funny and that rape jokes are unacceptable. If a supporter hears someone spreading dangerous myths about sexual assault—like that a girl is asking for it if she wears revealing clothes or that no does not always mean no—he or she can explain why these myths are wrong and dangerous. If a supporter hears someone gossiping about a sexual assault victim, he or she can explain to the person why sharing this story is a cruel boundary violation. Never let people trivialize this kind of talk by saying that boys will be boys or that this is just harmless locker-room talk.

In cases like this speaking out can feel awkward, and supporters might get some very negative reactions. However, when enough people make these everyday interventions, dangerous attitudes that normalize sexual assault will change.

There are many other things that supporters can do to help change dangerous attitudes about sexual assault and to help educate people about the importance of boundaries and consent. For example, a supporter can write an article or an editorial in a school newspaper about the topic or get involved with a local group that helps abuse survivors.

Standing in solidarity with survivors can mean offering help directly to individuals, but it can also mean working collectively with others to make society a safer place for everyone. Think of how successful the #MeToo tweets were at helping change cultural attitudes. Individually, each tweet was just a 280-character statement by one person, but together, all of those tweets made a huge impact. Everyday supporters have the power to foster societal change.

SOURCE NOTES

Introduction: #MeToo and You

1. Quoted in Jessica Bennett and Daniel Jones, "45 Stories of Sex and Consent on Campus," *New York Times*, May 10, 2018. www.nytimes.com.
2. Rape, Abuse & Incest National Network, "Sexual Harassment," July 25, 2018. www.rainn.org.
3. Quoted in Wendy Lu, "What #MeToo Means to Teenagers," *New York Times*, April 19, 2018. www.nytimes.com.

Chapter One: A Brief History of the #MeToo Movement

4. Cas (@Cassi0piea), "My daughter is experiencing her first bout with sexual harassment," Twitter, November 8, 2017, 11:05 p.m. https://twitter.com/Cassi0piea/status/928488693542748161.
5. Quoted in Nicole Carroll, "Tarana Burke on the Power of Empathy, the Building Block of the Me Too Movement," *USA Today*, August 19, 2020. www.usatoday.com.
6. Chanel Miller, *Know My Name: A Memoir*. New York: Penguin, 2020, p. 241.
7. Quoted in *New York Times*, "Transcript: Donald Trump's Taped Comments About Women," October 8, 2016. www.nytimes.com.
8. Quoted in Sophie Tatum, "Women's March on Washington: What You Need to Know," CNN, January 17, 2017. www.cnn.com.
9. Quoted in Perrie Samoton, "Madonna's Women's March Speech Was Too Brutal for TV—Here's Every Word," *Glamour*, January 21, 2017. www.glamour.com.
10. Alyssa Milano (@Alyssa_Milano), "If you've been sexually harassed or assaulted," Twitter, October 15, 2017, 3:21 p.m. https://twitter.com/alyssamilano/status/919659438700670976?lang=en.
11. Lily S. Axelrod (@LilySAxelrod), "Don't think I know a single woman who hasn't been sexually harassed at work, school, or on the street," Twitter, October 15, 2017, 3:44 p.m. https://twitter.com/lilysaxelrod/status/919665200046989314.

12. JustCate (@CatMilspo), "As a sixth grader, a group of boys held me against a wall," Twitter, October 15, 2017, 3:28 p.m. https://twitter.com/catmilspo/status/919661373814136832.
13. Allison Tolman (@Allison_Tolman), "Crowded tram at Disney, sat a row behind my family," Twitter, October 15, 2017, 7:50 p.m. https://twitter.com/allison_tolman/status/919727186579415040?lang=ar-x-fm.
14. Quoted in Me Too (@VocalizeMeToo), "When I was in high school it was not safe for me to walk to class by myself," Twitter, December 8, 2017, 11:29 p.m. https://twitter.com/VocalizeMeToo/status/939366376308985857.
15. Dina Ley (@dinachka82), "I'm a teacher in an urban high school and sexual harassment in our hallways," Twitter, November 9, 2017, 5:48 p.m. https://twitter.com/dinachka82/status/928771251409178625?ref_src=twsrc%5Etfw.
16. Quoted in Phil Hornshaw, "Read Oprah's Full Golden Globes #MeToo #TIMESUP Speech," The Wrap, January 7, 2018. www.thewrap.com.
17. Najwa Zebian (@najwazebian), "When you say #metoo, you're no longer alone in the struggle to be heard," Twitter, October 24, 2017, 11:15 a.m. https://twitter.com/najwazebian/status/922858986608750592.

Chapter Two: Boundaries in the #MeToo Era

18. Julia Smith, "My First Boyfriend," Youth Communication, 2023. https://youthcomm.org.
19. Sherri Gordon, "What Teens Need to Know About Boundaries," Verywell Family, July 26, 2021. www.verywellfamily.com.
20. Quoted in Brook, "Setting Boundaries: Cassie's Story," 2023. www.brook.org.uk.
21. Love Is Respect, "How to Create Boundaries in Romantic Relationships," 2023. www.loveisrespect.org.
22. Sharon Martin, "How to Set Boundaries with Kindness," Psych Central, January 25, 2019. https://psychcentral.com.
23. Shawn M. Burn, "What to Do When Someone Pushes Your Boundaries," *Presence of Mind* (blog), *Psychology Today*, August 22, 2022. www.psychologytoday.com.
24. Love Is Respect, "How to Set Boundaries," 2023. www.loveisrespect.org.

Chapter Three: Consent in the #MeToo Era

25. Quoted in Bennett and Jones, "45 Stories of Sex and Consent on Campus."

26. Rape, Abuse & Incest National Network, "What Consent Looks Like," October 30, 2020. www.rainn.org.
27. Quoted in Jaclyn Friedman and Jessica Valenti, *Yes Means Yes: Visions of Female Sexual Power and a World Without Rape*. New York: Hachette, 2019, pp. 2–3.
28. Quoted in Rape, Abuse & Incest National Network, "Isabella's Story," February 3, 2021. www.rainn.org.
29. Planned Parenthood, "Sexual Consent," 2023. www.plannedparenthood.com.
30. Emily Linden, "How to Say 'No' in the Middle of a Hookup Without Feeling Awkward About It," *Teen Vogue*, May 18, 2016. www.teenvogue.com.
31. Quoted in MTV News Staff, "Enthusiastic Consent Is Changing How We Have Sex," MTV, April 3, 2019. www.mtv.com.
32. Planned Parenthood, "How Do I Talk About Consent?," 2023. www.plannedparenthood.org.
33. Planned Parenthood, "How Do I Talk About Consent?"
34. Quoted in Bennett and Jones, "45 Stories of Sex and Consent on Campus."

Chapter Four: Boundaries and Consent: How to Support Others

35. Quoted in Emily Wang, "Sarah Hyland Shares Story of Being Sexually Assaulted," *Teen Vogue*, September 28, 2018. www.teenvogue.com.
36. Quoted in Kristen Dold, "I Was Raped—but I Didn't Report It. Here's Why," *Women's Health*. www.womenshealthmag.com.
37. Maryland Coalition Against Sexual Assault, "Victim Blaming Fact Sheet," 2022. https://mcasa.org.
38. Lori Bednarchik, "What Do I Do/Say If Someone Tells Me That They Have Been Sexually Assaulted," Campuspeak, 2018. https://campuspeak.com.
39. Penn State Student Affairs, "Support a Friend," 2022. https://studentaffairs.psu.edu.
40. Susan Storm, "10 Things Not to Say to a Sexual Abuse Survivor," Psychology Junkie, August 8, 2015. www.psychologyjunkie.com.
41. Storm, "10 Things Not to Say to a Sexual Abuse Survivor."
42. Rape, Abuse & Incest National Network, "Practicing Active Bystander Intervention," August 13, 2021. www.rainn.org.

WAYS FOR SUPPORTERS TO TAKE ACTION

Being a supporter is not just about helping individuals—it's about taking actions to try to make things better for communities and for society as a whole. Here are some ways that you can take action.

1. Write an article or editorial for your school newspaper about boundaries, consent, or related issues.

2. Submit an editorial for publication to a local newspaper about boundaries, consent, or related issues.

3. Does your school have a sex education program that includes information about boundaries and consent? If you think it should have more, talk to teachers, administrators, or school board members.

4. What kinds of policies does your school district have to fight sexual assault and harassment? If you think these can be improved in some way, talk to teachers, administrators, or school board members.

5. If you think your school needs better sex education or policies to fight sexual harassment and assault, write a petition and ask students to sign it.

6. Have conversations with other students about what they think should be done to fight sexual harassment and assault in your school.

7. Get involved in a student club that addresses issues like boundaries, consent, or sexual violence. If there isn't one in your school, start one.

8. Make posters about sexual harassment and assault or about boundaries and consent. Get permission to display these posters in school.

9. If you are an artist, musician, or creative writer, incorporate themes about boundaries, consent, sexual harassment, and sexual assault into your work. Consider displaying your art in your school or in another public place.

10. What kinds of policies does your community have to fight sexual assault and harassment? If you think these are insufficient, talk to a city council member. You can try to get the issue on the agenda for a community discussion.

11. Get involved with local organizations such as women's shelters.

12. Support political candidates who take issues like sexual assault and sexual harassment seriously. Volunteer to work on their campaigns, and if you are old enough, vote for them.

ORGANIZATIONS AND WEBSITES

Planned Parenthood
www.plannedparenthood.org
Planned Parenthood, the nation's largest women's health provider, has extensive information on its website about sexual consent. Planned Parenthood created the FRIES model of consent—an acronym for "freely given, reversible, informed, enthusiastic, and specific."

Rape, Abuse & Incest National Network (RAINN)
www.rainn.org
RAINN is the nation's largest anti–sexual violence organization. Its website has extensive information about sexual violence, consent, laws, and other topics, including survivor stories. RAINN operates the National Sexual Assault Hotline at (800) 656-4673 and can help survivors and their allies find local resources.

Stop Sexual Assault in Schools
https://stopsexualassaultinschools.org
Stop Sexual Assault in Schools created the #MeTooK12 Campaign to increase awareness of the prevalence of sexual assault and harassment in elementary, middle, and high schools. The website has tool kits for schools and information for students on how to cope with and fight sexual harassment.

Stop the Hurt
https://stopthehurt.org
Stop the Hurt—a project of the Hays-Caldwell Women's Center—offers educational resources to help people develop healthy relationships based on respect, consent, and equality. In addition to informative articles and links to resources, the website has quizzes that are fun and informative.

UnSlut Project
www.unslutproject.com
The UnSlut project is a space where people can share their experiences with sexual harassment and sexual bullying. Users can read stories and anonymously submit their own.

FOR FURTHER RESEARCH

Books

Leah Aguirre, *The Girl's Guide to Relationships, Sexuality & Consent: Tools to Help Teens Stay Safe, Empowered & Confident*. Oakland, CA: New Harbinger, 2022.

Halley Bondy, *#MeToo and You: Everything You Need to Know About Consent, Boundaries, and More*. Minneapolis, MN: Zest, 2021.

Cheryl M. Bradshaw, *Real Talk About Sex & Consent: What Every Teen Needs to Know*. Oakland, CA: Instant Help, 2020.

Tarana Burke, *Unbound: My Story of Liberation and the Birth of the Me Too Movement*. New York: Flatiron, 2021.

Donna Freitas, *The Big Questions Book of Sex and Consent*. Montclair, NJ: Levine Querido, 2020.

Jodi Kantor and Megan Twohey, *She Said: Breaking the Sexual Harassment Story That Helped Ignite a Movement*. New York: Penguin, 2019.

Internet Sources

Leah Asmelash, "In 5 Years of #MeToo, Here's What's Changed—and What Hasn't," CNN, October 27, 2022. www.cnn.com.

Anna Brown, "More than Twice as Many Americans Support than Oppose the #MeToo Movement," Pew Research Center, September 29, 2022. www.pewresearch.org.

Sherri Gordon, "How to Support a Victim of Sexual Assault," Verywell Mind, November 22, 2022. www.verywellmind.com.

New Jersey Coalition Against Sexual Violence, "Men as Allies in Sexual Assault Prevention: Fact Sheet," 2018. https://njcasa.org.

INDEX

Note: Boldface page numbers indicate illustrations.

Access Hollywood video, 11
active bystanders, 50–51
affirmative consent, 32, 40
  see also enthusiastic consent
allyship, 43
Antioch University, 40

belittling, as emotional coercion, 34–35
Belknap, Joanne, 44
boundaries
  as changeable, 25
  communicating, 26–27
  defining, 23–24
  enforcing, 28
  #MeToo and awareness of, 18–19
  nonnegotiable, 24
  physical *vs.* emotional, 21
  secondary, 24–25
  setting, 20
  special importance for girls, 20–21
boundary pushing, 28–30
Burke, Tarana, 9, **10**, 14
Burn, Shawn M., 29

Centers for Disease Control and Prevention, 6
Cho, Margaret, 34, **35**
Clinton, Hillary, 11
coercion, 7, 31
  definition of, 34
  emotional, 34–36
  enthusiastic consent is free from, 37–38
communication
  active listening and, 46
  of boundaries, 4, 26–27
  of consent, 38–41
  open, 41
consensual relationships, boundaries in, 7
consent
  blanket, 40
  communicating, 38–41
  legal capacity to, 32–33
  as reversible, 37
  as specific, 36–37
Conyers, John, 16

Daily Beast (website), 11
deal breakers, 24

Eichenberg, Maddy, 6
emotional boundaries, 22–23
emotional coercion, 34
  forms of, 34–36
Engle, Gigi, 37–38
enthusiastic consent, 32, 37–38

Facebook (social media platform), 12, 14
Franken, Al, 16

Gordon, Sherri, 20

guilt, as form of emotional coercion, 34–35

Hyland, Sarah, 43, 44–45

informed consent, 32
lying/withholding information and, 33

Keillor, Garrison, 16
kissing, 6

Lady Gaga, 15
Love Is Respect, 22–23, 30

Martin, Sharon, 27
Maryland Coalition Against Sexual Assault, 45
#MeTooK12 Campaign, 17, 18
#MeToo movement, 6, 8
global reach of, 12
origin of, 9
tweets from teenagers/children, 15–16
Milano, Alyssa, 13–14, **14**

National Domestic Violence Hotline, 30
National Sexual Violence Resource Center, 6, 7
New Yorker (magazine), 13
New York Times (newspaper), 11, 13
"no means no" phrase, 36

Paltrow, Gwyneth, 13
Palumbo, Laura, 43
physical boundaries, 21–22
Planned Parenthood, 37, 39, 40, 58

rape
definition of, 6
percentage of high school juniors victims of, 7
Rape, Abuse & Incest National Network (RAINN), 6, 32, 50, 58

sexual assault
definition of, 6
speaking out against, 51–52
sexual harassment
definition of, 6
earlier generations tolerated, 8
Shook, Teresa, 11–12
Smith, Julia, 20
solidarity, with survivors
allyship and, 43
by being active bystander, 50–51
listening and, 46–48
by speaking out, 51–52
ways to show, 42
Spacey, Kevin, 16
Stop Assault in Public Schools, 17 [ED: these 2 sound like the same organization]
Stop Sexual Assault in Schools, 58
Stop the Hurt, 58
Storm, Susan, 47, 48
street harassment/public harassment, 6, 50–51

Tambor, Jeffrey, 16
Thrush, Glenn, 16
time boundaries, 23
touching, 6
Trump, Donald, 11
Turner, Brock, 9–10, 11

Twitter (social media platform), 8
  spread of #MeToo posts on, 14–15

UnSlut Project, 58

victims
  avoiding minimizing experience of, 48
  blaming, 44–45
  finding resources for, 49–50
  importance of believing, 43–44
  listening to, 44–45
  of recent assault, helping, 49
  showing solidarity with, 42–43

Weinstein, Harvey, 13, 16, **17**
Winfrey, Oprah, 16–17
Women's March, 11
Wood, Evan Rachel, 15
workplace harassment
  forms of, 6
  impacts of #MeToo movement on awareness of, 16–17

PICTURE CREDITS

Cover: Naypong Studio/Shutterstock.com

5: Sundry Photography/Shutterstock.com
10: lev radin/Shutterstock.com
14: Jamie Lamor Thompson/Shutterstock.com
17: lev radin/Shutterstock.com
22: antoniodiaz/Shutterstock.com
25: LightField Studios/Shutterstock.com
29: StratfordProductions/Shutterstock.com
33: Max kegfire/Shutterstock.com
35: Kathy Hutchins/Shutterstock.com
39: VGstockstudio/Shutterstock.com
44: Jacob Lund/Shutterstock.com
47: MDV Edwards/Shutterstock.com
51: MDV Edwards/Shutterstock.com

ABOUT THE AUTHOR

Naomi Rockler, PhD, is an educational freelance writer who writes nonfiction and fiction books for teenagers. She lives in Minnesota with her husband and daughter.